The Ghost Stallion

LAURA E. WILLIAMS

HENRY HOLT AND COMPANY

NEW YORK

Thanks

to Marti Karau who knows so much,

to Kris Till who lived out there,

to my SCBWI and RWA writers' groups who critique with love,

to my agent, Edy Selman, who never lets me get away with anything,

and to Christy Ottaviano who has 20/20 vision.

Henry Holt and Company, LLC, *Publishers since 1866*
115 West 18th Street, New York, New York 10011

Henry Holt is a registered trademark of
Henry Holt and Company, LLC
Copyright © 1999 by Laura E. Williams. All rights reserved.
Published in Canada by Fitzhenry & Whiteside Ltd.,
195 Allstate Parkway, Markham, Ontario L3R 4T8.

Library of Congress Cataloging-in-Publication Data
Williams, Laura E. The ghost stallion / Laura E. Williams.
p.   cm.   Summary: In 1959 in Oregon, thirteen-year-old Mary Elizabeth rides
with her father to kill the wild stallion that is luring away horses from their
ranch and ruining their livelihood, but she secretly wants to save its life.
[1. Wild horses—Fiction.   2. Horses—Fiction.   3. Ranch life—Oregon—Fiction.
4. Oregon—Fiction.   5. Fathers and daughters—Fiction.]   I. Title.
PZ7.W666584Gh   1999   [Fic]—dc21   99-24686

ISBN 0-8050-6193-2 / First Edition—1999
Printed in the United States of America on acid-free paper. ∞

1   3   5   7   9   10   8   6   4   2

I dedicate this book with love
to my wonderful aunts and uncles, past and present—

Marguerite Williams
Bob and Margaret Spurrier
Gayle and Brent Welling

The Ghost Stallion

chapter 1

When Sunny died, Pa wrapped one end of a thick, rusty chain around her neck. He hooked the other end up to his tractor and dragged her out of the barn.

Uncle Leroy wanted to skin her. "Make a great seat cover for my truck," he said, shifting his toothpick from one side of his mouth to the other, real smooth.

My five-year-old sister started bawling. "Can't skin my pony," Nellie cried, her tears making clean streaks down her dusty cheeks. "Gotsta bury her with her skin on."

"She ain't a pony," Uncle Leroy growled. "She's a horse. And she ain't yours, she's your pappy's. And he ain't burying her, he's selling her to the chicken feeders."

Nellie cried harder, and she screamed above the roar of the tractor.

"Hush," I said, patting her yellow hair like Ma used to do. "Hush." I couldn't help wishing I had yellow hair, too. Like Pa and Ma. But my hair is as black as the sludge on the bottom of Trumans' cow pond. Maybe even blacker.

Sometimes I catch Pa staring at it as if he's wondering where it came from. I sure don't look like his side of the family.

"Ain't gonna skin Sunny, is you, Pa?" Nellie cried when Pa turned off the tractor.

He jumped down from the high seat and scooped her up, swinging her in his arms till her tears dried. "Now who been filling your ears about the chicken feeders?" Pa asked. Only he twirled her around when he talked, so I really only heard, "Now . . . filling . . . about . . . chicken . . ." But I knew what he said 'cause I'm good at figuring out stuff like that.

Uncle Leroy spit his toothpick into the dirt and ground it like a lit cigarette with the pointy toe of his boot. Slouching as always, he shuffled away, muttering to himself under his breath.

I looked over at Sunny, lying on her side. Flies buzzed around her eyes and mouth. Only now, Sunny was dead and the flies didn't bother her no more.

"Girl, you telling little precious about the chicken feeders?" Pa asked me.

"Nah—was Uncle Leroy." It stung me like a bee how he called me *girl* and Nellie *little precious*. Only, she *was* little and she *was* precious most of the time. Everyone said so.

Pa glared at me. Looked like he was going to say something more, but Nellie was hugging him around the neck, begging to be carried into the house for some of Auntie's gravy and biscuits. He forgot about me and carried her down the path from the barn, him ducking his head low to hear what she was saying, them laughing and giggling together.

Nellie looks like Ma with her pretty little face and narrow shoulders, but she surely takes after Pa's side of the family when it comes to everything else. They even laugh the same.

Pa carried her up the worn back stairs and through the screen door, which slammed closed behind them. Roses climbed up over the door like a fountain of flowers as they did every summer. Ma had planted them when she first moved here.

The sun was just a wash of orange on the horizon, like one of Ma's watercolor paintings that Pa kept up in the attic. I squatted down next to Sunny and waved my hands to shoo away the flies, but they were thick and stubborn and didn't pay me no mind. I stroked her cheek anyway, like I used to when she nuzzled my hand for an apple. Her neck was all stretched out funny from being hauled from the barn. After supper Pa would finish the job, loading her up onto the truck and driving her over to Mr. Semple's place. Didn't know what Mr. Semple did with dead horses, and I didn't figure on asking, either. Maybe he did sell them to the men who made chicken feed or to the glue factory. But some things, I reckon, are better not to know.

"Bye, Sunny," I whispered. "I loved riding you."

I started riding Sunny about ten years ago, when I was no more than three years old. She was a smallish quarter horse, barely fourteen hands, but she had big intentions. She never ran fast enough to make it to

Mr. Semple's racing stable, but she was a good cutting horse in her time, and she bred real fine. Her sons Alonso and Mighty Comfort went on to become champions for Mr. Semple. Sunny didn't have no purses or trophies, but that didn't matter to me. I learned to ride on her. Learned to fall off, too.

I wanted tears to come, to fill my eyes like they did Nellie's all the time. I wanted my tears to fall on Sunny so she'd know how much I loved her, so she'd know how much my heart ached for her being gone. I wanted to cry so bad, I even pinched myself on the arm real hard, but I didn't have no tears in me.

After awhile the smell of Auntie's gravy made my stomach rumble like an old wagon and overpowered my longing to cry. I gave Sunny one last pat on the neck, then headed to the house.

—

We lived in a cracked and peeling gray farmhouse. It was a narrow house with skinny windows and a back door that let in only one person at a time. We never used the front door for nothing more than hanging a bridle or a sweater on the tarnished doorknob.

Just before I turned up the path to the house, I looked out over the near fields. They were purple-blue in the late light, and the gentle breeze that always came with night rippled them so they looked like an ocean. Not that I'd ever seen an ocean, but I'd read about them plenty in the books Ma brought with her from the city. She had more books than Miss Whipple at the schoolhouse.

Then, out beyond the ocean of grass, the sage-brush and dead place started and ran right up to the ridge of mountains far off. Ma called it the dead place because sometimes we found dead cattle out there, the hide sucked up against their bones.

I squinted. I didn't have no hope of seeing the ghost stallion, but I looked anyway. Course he wasn't really a ghost—he was flesh and bone, with blood running through him so wild that nobody tried to break him like the other mustangs. I didn't want to tame him, just wanted to see him wild and free in the distance.

I saw nothing, as usual.

With a sigh I turned up the brick walk, the uneven blocks shifting under my feet. Ma had wanted the bricks. She said it was proper. Pa said it was a waste of money, but he'd laid each brick himself. Used to be they were even and smooth, but time had let the weeds grow and the corners crumble. Now Pa didn't even walk on the bricks. He wore a path in the grass right alongside the proper one. In the last nine months since Ma'd been gone, he even talked about digging it up, but he hadn't yet got around to it. I was glad. I liked the walkway. Reminded me of Ma.

I stepped into the house and took off my boots by the door. Pa and Uncle Leroy ate beside the radio in the living room, and Nellie, Auntie, and I sat at the wooden table in the kitchen. Auntie always set the table with silver, mostly gone black with tarnish, and used a real cloth table covering. Sometimes she picked some wildflowers and put them in a jam jar in the center, but she wasn't clever with designing like Ma was. Ma could've taken the ugliest weeds you ever saw and made them into a wreath you'd be proud to wear to church.

"There you are," Auntie said, heaving off the rickety chair and waddling to the stove to fix me a plate. "Wash up," she reminded me before I could sit down.

I scrubbed my hands and face at the kitchen sink. The water was cold, pumped by hand to the large cistern, then gravity-fed into the house.

"Wash up, whether you need it or not," was Auntie's rule. Even Pa and Uncle Leroy had to obey her on that law. That one and the one about closing the outhouse door so's the critters didn't get in and fall down the hole. No one liked the job of digging them out.

I sat down at the table, and Auntie examined my hands. They were clean, like new buds sticking off two brown branches. I washed my hands, but the cleaning stopped at the wrists. Never did nobody no good to have clean arms.

I glanced over at Nellie. She always had clean everything. Even her dusty, tear-streaked cheeks were now shiny and red. And her arms were clean clear up to the short sleeves on her shirt. Someone had brushed her yellow hair, and it looked all silky and fuzzy at the same time. Like an angel. Pa's little precious angel. But I couldn't hate her for that. It wasn't her fault I had black hair.

I dug into my biscuit and gravy. Even though I started last, I knew I'd finish first. Nellie was too slow and careful, cutting and chewing each piece like it was something special. Could take her all night. And Auntie took some time over her three heaping helpings. Pa and Uncle Leroy washed down every bite with a chug of beer as they talked about what needed to be done the next day, so it took them longer, too.

"Slow down," Auntie said. "That's no way for a lady to eat."

Ma used to say that to me all the time, and I tried real hard to please her. I wanted to be a lady, talking proper and smelling like roses.

Now that Ma was gone, Auntie took up her lines: "Slow down. Talk softer. Don't smile with so much teeth showing—you look like a horse." But coming from Auntie, it didn't seem the same. Hard to be polite when the one telling you is a woman three times too big wearing clothes two times too small, who eats with her mouth open on account of she can't breathe so good through her nose. But she does use a napkin real dainty. Ma taught her that.

"Mmph," Auntie said, dropping her fork and grabbing her elbow at the same time. Her face puckered with pain and she shook her head. "Storm coming."

"Is not," Nellie said between tiny bites. "Daddy read in the almanac that there'd only be dry weather for another week at least."

"You believe your almanac," Auntie retorted, returning her attention to her plate but still rubbing her elbow, "and I'll believe my aching bones. They telling me a big storm is on its way. I hurt so bad, I think I'll have to lay abed."

Funny thing about Auntie, she was always wrong. About the weather, anyhow. She couldn't forecast rain or snow or even a sunny day if the sun was shining. But that didn't mean nothing. One time when her bones ached so bad and she had to go to bed, the ghost stallion stole five of Pa's mares. And another time, Pa told us Ma died.

chapter 2

After supper Auntie started to scrub the dishes. Uncle Leroy stood by the sink with her, drying the plates and glasses and silver as she handed them over. Every once in a while their arms rubbed together and they seemed to press against each other, like they enjoyed the contact. Sometimes they even sat on the sagging couch next to the radio and held hands. Or if Uncle Leroy was in a fit, Auntie rubbed his back all smooth till the meanness slid out of him. Only she could calm him.

Ma used to rub my back and brush the tangles from my hair. It felt good to be touched. When I saw Auntie and Uncle Leroy touching, it hurt my heart in a way I didn't know how to ease.

I slipped outside so as not to interrupt them. Nellie

was bundled in front of the radio, listening to some show with lots of laughter.

Outside, I watched Pa getting ready to haul Sunny away. He stood still for a moment, his hands shoved into the pockets of his jeans. The frayed edges on the cutoff sleeves of his shirt fluttered against his arms, which were wiry strong and brown as dirt from the sun. He kept his boots planted wide and his legs bowed out a little, like mine did. Curse of the saddle, he called it.

He looked down at the dead horse like he was praying or something. Only far as I knew, Pa never said a prayer in his life. Then he snorted and spit at the fence, hitting the crossbars dead center.

I never seen Pa cry, even after what Ma did. Only sometimes his voice gets all thick sounding, like he's choking on a wad of hay, and he snorts and spits a lot. He never snorted for me, though. Not even when I fell off Sunny and broke my arm.

I was just about to go help Pa when Uncle Leroy stepped out of the house. I hung back. Sometimes Pa and I could work with the horses without talking, like we knew what each other was thinking. But when Uncle Leroy was around, static filled the air, and me and Pa just growled at each other.

I turned the other way and went to my evening chores. Had to check the water troughs, and do the haying, and fill the oat bin. I put out milk for the kittens and wrestled with the mutts who hung around the barn. By the time I was done, Sunny was in the truck and Uncle Leroy had driven off. Pa was out in the middle pasture, standing quiet and looking toward the mountains like he did every night. I wondered if he was looking for the ghost stallion, too.

Crack of gunfire woke me up the next morning. Not often we heard gunfire, 'cept if Pa had to kill a lame horse or if he was hunting an ornery badger. The sound rang against the distant mountains and came back like it didn't want to go away.

From my bed I could see out the window to the stable and the back corrals and the fields beyond. Morning light made everything look gray, and there was Pa, like a misty ghost, shaking his rifle in the air and stomping his feet.

I saw right away that one of the back lodgepole fences had been crushed and the mares, ripe for breeding, had run off.

"The ghost stallion," I whispered, wishing I had seen him.

I jammed myself into my jeans and boots, pulled on a T-shirt and a thick flannel shirt. It was an old one of Pa's but since I'm so tall and have shoulders broad enough for a boy, the shirt fit me. I charged out of the house, reaching Pa with barely a breath left.

"It was him, wasn't it, Pa?"

"I'm going to kill that devil horse."

"No, Pa. Some people trying to protect the wild horses. They won't like it if you kill one." I didn't need to tell him I was one of those people. He knew. Besides, I didn't hold no influence over him.

"Those do-gooders going to give me back my mares and foals I lost? Only way I'll git 'em back is if I take care of this myself." He started to stomp toward the house.

I grabbed the sleeve of his worn work shirt. "You're not really going to kill him, are you, Pa?"

He shook my hand free. "Why shouldn't I? It ain't

right that he steals from me and I can't do nothing about it, is it? What am I supposed to do?" He might have said something more, but a truck drove down the drive toward us.

I recognized the truck. Easy to do since we didn't have many neighbors. It was a brand-new Ford. Red with shiny wheels. Only Mr. Semple could afford a truck like that.

The truck slammed to a stop, and Mr. Semple jumped out of the cab. His thin face was pulled tight over his skull like them cattle out in the dead place. We called him Bones behind his back.

"Goddamned devil horse," he cursed, taking off his hat and flapping it against his skinny leg. "Goddamned ghost stallion. I'm going to kill that son of a—" Then he saw me and stopped. His lips moved for a bit, with nothing coming out. "That danged horse took six of my very best mares. Six!"

Pa nodded vigorously. "Took four here. Out on the north field."

"Any of them mine?" Semple asked sharply.

Pa shook his head, his shoulders sagging. Mostly he bred and trained for Mr. Semple, but he had some of his own horses he was trying to train so eventually he wouldn't have to work for someone else. But if the ghost stallion kept stealing his stock that was never gonna happen.

"I just got back the other mares he took last winter," Mr. Semple said, interrupting my thoughts. "Couldn't git *him*, though. That stallion's just laughing at us."

Pa sighed. "He beat down the fence and wire like it was nothing."

I winced. The wire was electrified. Even though it was smooth as fishing line and not barbed like the drift fencing the cattle ranchers used, it could cut like a knife.

I remembered the last time the ghost stallion had come for a visit. One of Mr. Semple's mares that Pa was training got tangled in the wire. Cut right through the pastern joint, just above the heel of the hoof. Horse bled to death before we could save her. Pa and Mr. Semple blamed the ghost stallion for that, but I didn't.

"I'm offering a reward," Mr. Semple said to Pa. "One hundred dollars to kill him."

"You can't kill him," I blurted out.

"He's a thief," Mr. Semple bit back before Pa could tell me to shut up. "Thieving's against the law, right? And criminals go to jail, right?"

I nodded, knowing he was trying to trick me.

"Ain't no horse jail, so we have to kill him." He said it like there was no more to say about it.

"But it ain't right to kill horses, even if they are wild," I argued. I didn't see Pa's hand till it smacked against my shoulder.

"Git to the house," he growled.

Arguing with Pa when it was just Pa was bad enough, but it wouldn't do me no better if I opened my mouth against him in front of a man like Mr. Semple. Still, I couldn't help saying under my breath, "What's wrong with wanting to be free?" as I walked away, slow as I could.

"Girl don't have no sense," Pa said, sounding sorry he knew me.

Mr. Semple snorted. "She's just a filly. She'll understand one day."

I didn't need to hear Pa say, "I doubt it," to know that's what he was thinking.

They kept talking, and their voices turned to faint mumbling. I was just to the back door of the house when Uncle Leroy thundered up on his horse. He must have been out chasing the ghost stallion. I laughed to myself, him thinking he even had a chance.

Then something quieter caught my eye. Another rider, only he wasn't thundering, just walking along, sitting on his horse like he was part of the animal between his legs.

I sat down on the step to watch. We hardly got strangers to these parts. Sometimes they came with fancy trucks, pulling horse trailers, looking to buy good stock for cheap. Usually, though, they got to Mr. Semple's and didn't come no farther. But I never saw anyone just ride up on a horse, looking like he didn't care whether he stopped or just kept riding.

The stranger appeared tall. Could see that even on the horse. Maybe taller than Mr. Semple, but not as skinny. He wore a black hat pulled low on his brow, but dark hair peeped out from under the brim.

The sky was getting lighter, and the misty shadows were turning to yellow and orange. But the stranger didn't seem to be any color at all 'cept for his pale face that glowed from under his hat.

Pa, Uncle Leroy, and Mr. Semple watched the stranger come toward them, slow as tree sap. Finally Pa couldn't stand the wait no longer, and he stepped up to meet him halfway, his rifle swinging forward like he was aiming to shoot the man. I knew Pa wasn't expecting no one, or I'd have heard something about it.

Uncle Leroy got off his horse. Him and Mr. Semple joined Pa, all three of them looking up at the stranger, only he wasn't looking at them. He was looking at the swing hanging from under the tree on the side of the house. Ma used to sit there for hours, gazing down the road toward the mountains.

I bumped down off the step on my rear and crept along the brick path, moving from tree to tree. There was something about this stranger that reminded me of someone.

"He's got a one-hundred-dollar reward on his head now," Mr. Semple was saying. "If you've got the time, we could use your help. Most of my hands are at an auction, and I can't spare the rest just now. So what do you say?"

The three men waited for the stranger to reply, only he didn't.

"Are you interested?" Mr. Semple said, like he couldn't stand the silence no more.

"Might be," the stranger said, his voice so soft, I almost didn't hear him.

"We're heading out now," Pa said. "Figure we'll find him in Smoky's Canyon."

"Ever found him there before?" the stranger asked.

"Nope," Pa said. "But that don't mean I won't this time."

The stranger didn't say anything.

Mr. Semple spoke up quick. "Bring him to me dead. The deader the better. One hundred bucks it'll get you."

"For each of us?" asked the stranger.

"Well, uh. Well, yes, dammit." He hit his hat on his leg again. Seems he did that a lot. "Worth it to get rid of that devil horse. One hundred each." He nodded firmly as if to agree with himself.

I cursed him under my breath. Auntie would have had a fit if she heard me. Ladies weren't supposed to swear. My mama was a lady, but it didn't do her no good. I swore again, careful not to be heard.

Mr. Semple clapped Pa on the shoulder and scooted like a daddy longlegs back over to his truck. "One hundred for each of you," he called out. "Bring me the bastard's tail."

The dew on the dirt road was already dried up, and the truck left a dusty cloud behind itself.

Pa fanned away a fly. He looked up at the stranger, shielding his eyes from the rising sun. "I'm Jim, and this here's my sister's husband, Leroy."

The stranger nodded, then Pa and Uncle Leroy waited for him to introduce himself.

"Well," Pa said, clearing his throat when the stranger said nothing, "let's eat and pack up. Join us?" he asked. "Evelyn, that's my sister, she'll cook us something, then we'll head out."

Uncle Leroy shook his head. "Evie's gone worked herself into another fit. Said she ain't getting out of bed today, no way, no how. Said a big storm's coming."

The stranger tipped his head back like he was looking for the coming storm. Only he didn't know Auntie's storms had nothing to do with the weather.

"Guess I'll join you for a bit," he said finally. "Not in any special hurry to get somewhere else."

"That devil horse stole all he's gonna get from me," Pa said, practically spitting out the words. "Mr. Semple wants the tail, and I'll take the head. Stuff it and mount it on the wall, I will."

I gasped and stepped out from behind my hiding tree. "Pa, you can't do that!"

All three of them turned to look at me. The stranger stared real hard. His eyes were as black as his boots.

"Can and will," Pa snapped back. "I told you to go inside—now git."

"No." I don't know why I said it, but the word just came out sharp like the crack of a whip.

For a long breath no one said nothing. The stranger kept staring at me. I stared back without blinking until my eyes started to burn. I had to blink a couple of times, and when I looked again, the stranger was staring off across the fields.

Then Pa exhaled slow and steady. "Girl, don't talk back to me ever."

"She needs to learn her a lesson," Uncle Leroy said.

I took a deep breath. "I—I want to come with you," I said.

"What are you talking about?" Pa snapped back.

"I want to go find the ghost stallion."

"Ghost stallion?" the stranger asked.

I turned to him. "On account of nobody ever seeing him up close," I explained quickly. "Never mind come near to catching him."

"He ain't no ghost." Uncle Leroy added, "Yet." He grinned at Pa, but Pa wasn't in no mood to snicker at a poor joke, so Leroy soured up again.

"Go cook us some breakfast," Pa ordered.

"You know I can't—" I started, but I stopped soon

as I saw Pa's face twist up like he was going to shout. I headed back to the house, not giving up on the idea of going with them.

—

Inside, I found some raw, ground-up cow in the gas-powered refrigerator, and since that was all I knew how to cook, I made us hamburgers for breakfast. Hamburgers on toast with lots of ketchup. What did they expect when I kept to the stables mostly? Auntie said I just got in the way in the kitchen and that Pa needed my help outside 'cause he depended on me. That always made me laugh, but Auntie swore it was true. I told her someday I'd save up and buy her some eyeglasses so she could see better.

"Whatcha doing in there?" Auntie called from her bedroom when I started to fry the meat.

"Cooking breakfast," I called back.

"But you don't know how to cook nothing but hamburgers."

"That's what we're having for breakfast." I flipped a couple of patties. They weren't round or anything, more like the shape of Texas—not that I ever been to Texas, but I seen it in an atlas at school.

Auntie found the strength to get up and close her door like she couldn't stand the thought of me in her kitchen.

That's how it was when Ma was around, too. Story was, Auntie and Uncle Leroy came to live with them the day after Ma and Pa got married. Ma couldn't cook more than a hard-boiled egg, so Auntie took over the kitchen, which suited Ma just fine. Gave her more time for her books and painting.

The funny thing about that story is that it changed a couple of times. I was born in 1946, June. One time Auntie said she moved here in 1947. I wondered how that could be if Auntie and Uncle Leroy moved in when Ma and Pa got married?

I asked Auntie about it once, but she pursed her lips tighter than a cider press. Wouldn't tell me nothing. She never said to ask Ma, but I knew that was the only place I'd get any answers, only I couldn't. I was afraid to know.

But ever since, I started to notice the differences in me—how my hair was dark, my fingers long and narrow, not like Pa's short, strong hands nor slim and delicate like Ma's. And how he treated Nellie as if she were his only daughter, especially since Ma was gone. Sometimes I wondered if I even had me a pa at all.

I was just through burning the toast when Nellie pranced in with her nose all scrunched up. "What's that stink?" she asked.

"Breakfast."

She looked in the frying pan. "I can't eat no cow for breakfast," she wailed. "And you burnt the toast."

"Not too bad," I said, scraping the black stuff off into the sink. "It'll taste just fine with lots of ketchup."

"I don't like ketchup."

"So put honey on it."

Just then Pa and Uncle Leroy stomped in. They took their boots off at the door like Ma was still around to care. Then they placed their hats on the side table. I waited for the stranger to clomp in after them, but I didn't hear nothing.

I set plates, all of them chipped but one, and served up the hamburgers and scraped toast.

"Where is he?" I asked, once everyone had been served.

"He's tending his horse," Pa said through a mouthful of food.

My stomach fluttered too much for me to eat.

When he came in, the stranger didn't clomp like Pa and Uncle Leroy—he stepped real nice, like a gentleman. And he even took off his boots and hat at the door like he knew Ma's rule. I hurried and brought him the good plate with his breakfast on it. I set it at his place just as he sat down.

"Looks real fine," he said, sounding like he wasn't lying.

No one ever said anything good about my cooking. I couldn't even say thank you, so I just hurried back to the counter and started to wash the skillet.

Nellie hadn't said anything since the stranger walked in. She sat at the table, her chin barely over the top of it, chewing her honey on toast real slow. After she swallowed a piece, she asked, "What's your name?"

The stranger put down his fork and leaned across the table. "And what's *your* name?"

She giggled. "Nellie."

"Now, isn't that a pretty name," the stranger said. "Pretty name for a pretty young lady." Then he put his hand up next to her ear and pulled it away. A shiny coin between his fingers seemed to come from inside her ear.

Nellie giggled harder, and the stranger smiled. I smiled, too. Couldn't help it.

"How'd you do that?" Nellie squealed when he handed her the penny.

He winked. "It's a secret, pretty girl," he whispered so everyone could hear.

As I scrubbed the pan harder, I wondered what other secrets he held in his hands. Even though I wasn't a baby like Nellie, I wished for some reason he'd pull a coin out of my ear.

"I'm pretty just like my ma," Nellie said proudly, flipping the coin from one hand to the other. "Only Ma's dead."

"Is she, now," the stranger said, his smile fading like a waning moon. "That's a shame." He bowed his head.

Pa cleared his throat. "So where you from?" I'm sure Pa asked just to change the conversation. He didn't like talking about Ma.

"Nowhere in particular," the stranger said, starting to eat again.

"No place to call home?" Uncle Leroy asked. I could tell by the way his eyes squinted at the stranger that he didn't like him much. Course Uncle Leroy didn't like many people far as I could tell.

"That's right," answered the stranger.

I rinsed off the pan, which was cleaner than I'd ever seen it, and dried it with the towel hanging under the window.

I kept looking at the stranger. He ate with his left hand, like I did. His fingers were long and flat, 'cept his pinkie, which turned in like he was drinking tea. I glanced down at my hands. I had a tea-drinking pinkie, too. His hair was flattened some from his hat, but the ends curled up like mine.

That's when I remembered a necklace Ma used to wear all the time. It was a silver heart that opened up. Inside, Ma kept a lock of hair. Never did tell me whose it was, but it was black as midnight, and it curled at the end like a dying leaf.

chapter 4

After breakfast I followed the men out to the barn. I breathed in the smell of grain and dung. Horseflies buzzed around me, looking to take a juicy bite, but I swatted them away with my hat. Mama cat and her four dusty kittens rubbed against my leg, begging me to scratch them. I couldn't refuse, even if they did make me sneeze.

I would have slept out here if Pa let me, but he said it wasn't proper, as if Ma were still around whispering in his ear. Only thing was, I thought maybe Ma *would* have let me sleep out here, closer to the horses and the land and the mountains.

I swung myself up onto one of the stall doors. "Can I come with you, Pa?"

"And get in the way?" Pa demanded, tightening the girth around Thunder's belly.

"I won't bother you," I promised, hopeful since he didn't say no right off.

"She just wants to scare the stallion before we can get him," Uncle Leroy said, yanking too hard on Jacko's halter.

I didn't say anything, since I couldn't outright deny it.

"Why not let her come?" muttered the stranger.

We all turned to look in his direction.

He didn't look at us, but fiddled some with the bit in his horse's mouth. "She can't do no harm. And she can cook for us."

"I cook better than she does," Uncle Leroy said with disgust. He was right, but I gave him a dirty look anyhow. He threw it right back at me, only harder and dirtier. I knew he cussed me under his breath sometimes, but I also knew he'd never do me no real harm. He just liked to growl like a mangy dog.

"I reckon it's none of my business, but maybe it's

time she learned," the stranger said. Satisfied with the bit, he moved to check the cinch.

Pa never actually said I could go, but he didn't say nothing when I saddled up old Blue. Maybe he knew I'd ride out after them no matter what. Or maybe it had something to do with what the stranger said.

Before we left, I ran to the house for a sweater. I snatched one from my bottom drawer and flung it over my shoulder. As I was leaving my room, I caught a glimpse of myself in the small mirror I had hanging from some braided horsehair next to my door. I didn't spend too much time looking at myself, like Nellie did, but seeing my hair swish by reminded me of Ma's locket.

I looked out into the hall. A rope hung down from the trapdoor in the ceiling.

I listened. The house was still. Nellie was singing to herself on the back step. Everyone was outside except Auntie, and she was probably asleep or aching too bad to know what was going on.

I stepped quiet over to the rope and tugged on it. The door slowly opened down. I knew I should let go of the rope and forget what I was thinking, but it was like some other spirit got ahold of my hand and wouldn't do what my mind told it to.

My heart thumped in my ears while I unfolded the stairs down to the floor. As quickly and quietly as I could, I climbed up until I was in the attic. I knew I had to hurry or Pa would leave without me.

Boxes and junk cluttered close to the opening. Most of it belonged to Ma. Pa had packed it all one night and stuffed it up here. He said he'd whip us good if he ever caught us poking through the boxes. I didn't know why he kept everything, why he didn't just burn it if he didn't want me and Nellie to have it. Didn't make no sense.

Still, it was there, all her stuff, sitting above our heads like an avalanche about to happen. Sometimes I dreamed it all came tumbling out of the attic and buried us in rose perfume and memories.

The dim light coming up from the stairs lit the space. I pulled one box nearer, and with my pocket-knife I cut loose the string holding it closed. I lifted the cardboard flaps and peered in. Pushing away the folds of silks and satins, I buried my hands deeper into the box. I was just about to give up and go on to the next one when my fingers brushed against the hard edge of Ma's jewelry box. I pulled it out, the nightgowns and slips falling away like ribbons of water.

Turning carefully on the narrow steps, I sat down and balanced the wooden box on my knees. I lifted the lid. The silver heart locket lay right on top. It felt warm like someone had just taken it off. I snapped it open. Hair dark as mine curled in the center. Dark as the stranger's. But I knew it wasn't my hair in the locket on account of Ma had it tucked in there way back when my hair was more the color of tanned leather. Seems every year it got darker. So whose lock of hair was it? And why had Ma kept it close to her heart all those years?

Downstairs, the back door banged open. "Girl! Get out here!"

My heart stopped beating. I knew he couldn't see me from the kitchen, and I prayed he stayed there. "I'm coming, Pa," I yelled back, closing the locket and looping the thin silver chain over my head. The heart swung down against my chest, and I dropped it under my shirt so no one would see it. With trembling fingers, I shut the jewelry box and placed it back in its cocoon of satins and silks.

When the back door slammed shut, I breathed a sigh of relief. As quietly as I could, I climbed down and let the attic stairs close up against the ceiling, then I dashed down another flight of stairs to the kitchen.

Auntie stood in her bedroom doorway, just off the kitchen. Clutching her arms to her middle, she stared at me like she knew what I'd just done. "Big storm," she whispered. Then she turned and went back into her room, shutting the door behind her.

I raced to the barn and rolled the sweater in a blanket and tarp and tied it onto the back of my saddle. I also grabbed a canteen and filled it with water.

We rode out, me waving to Nellie as she sat on the love seat swing Pa had rigged for Ma. Nellie wasn't lying when she said she looked just like Ma, small and delicate like a pretty doll.

The only way I knew I was Ma's girl was my eyes. Not sky blue like Pa's and Nellie's, but a shade closer to the mountains at sunset. Dreamy violet, Ma used to call it.

Pa and Uncle Leroy took the lead. The stranger followed, and I trailed him. I watched out for the ghost stallion, wishing I'd see him but praying I wouldn't and all the time wondering what was stronger, the praying or the wishing. But neither one of them ever worked. I had wished and prayed for lots of things—that Ma wasn't gone, or that I had hair the color of straw, or that Pa loved me. Never did me any good, all those wasted wishes and prayers.

We rode like that all day until the stranger found the hoofprints. I'd already spotted some stud piles, but I sure never mentioned them.

It wasn't hard to follow the trail. Sure enough, he and his mares headed right for Smoky's Canyon. I wondered how Pa knew where the stallion would go and how I would stop him from killing the horse.

We finally stopped when the mountains looked like dreamy violet.

Uncle Leroy and the stranger hobbled the horses while Pa unpacked some food he brought along. Dinner was chunks of crusty bread and cheddar cheese.

Pa made a little fire to heat water for the coffee. The coffee and woodsmoke smelled good. No one spoke. It was silent except for the crackling of the sticks as they burst apart in the fire.

With the sun gone, the chill sucked any heat out of me. I pulled on my sweater and wrapped the blanket around my shoulders, then the tarp to keep off the morning dew.

I lay down on my back and stared up at the stars. Ma used to tell me how you couldn't see any stars in the big cities like New York and Chicago on account of the many lights. But out here on the range, with only a campfire, the stars were packed so thick and bright, it looked like a herd of wild horses had just galloped across the sky, kicking up enough star dust for one million wishes.

Me and Ma, we used to sit for hours on the rail, lifting our faces to the night sky. She taught me constellations like Ursa Major and Minor, and Draco the dragon, and Orion with his two hunting dogs at his heels. We made wishes on shooting stars.

I asked her once why her and Pa never sat out looking at the night sky.

"He doesn't understand about stars and wishes," she said. "He only believes in things that give him blisters and an aching back. But he's a good man, a hard worker. He's just not a dreamer."

I was glad to hear it. I wanted Ma all to myself. Nellie was too young to sit still and watch the sky move, and Pa . . . Well, sometimes I felt sorry for Pa, me taking his place next to Ma all the time. Maybe that's why he didn't like me much. Or maybe it was something else.

I rolled onto my side, facing the fire. My left hand crept up under my sweater and curled around the locket.

The stranger sat across the fire from me, and I could see his face through the flickering flames.

I tugged on the chain around my neck, wondering if the hair in the locket could possibly belong to the stranger. And what I would do if it did.

chapter

Can't say what woke me the next morning. Could've been the hard ground. I was used to my lumpy, soft mattress at home. Or maybe it was the stranger staring at me. I could feel his gaze even before I opened my eyes. And when I did open them and looked his way, he was pretending I wasn't even there.

I watched him close, looking for bits of me in him besides the pinkies and the curling hair. Did I put my hat on like that? Did I squint into the rising sun just that way? Did my voice roll like hills, all smooth up and down?

He finally looked over at me as he pulled a pouch from his back pocket. With a grin that flashed his white teeth, he started to roll a cigarette.

"You smoke?" he asked.

I shook my head. "Not yet," I said, quietly in case Pa was listening as he dug a small sack of ground coffee out of his saddlebag.

The stranger jerked his head for me to come closer to him. I glanced at Pa, but he was fumbling like the coffee was missing or something, so I crept over to the stranger, pulling my blanket and tarp along with me.

He handed me a small, thin piece of paper, then he dribbled some sweet-smelling tobacco onto it. "Roll it up like this," he said.

I watched his fingers rub back and forth, back and forth. But when I tried it, the paper wrinkled and the tobacco scattered on the ground. The stranger laughed softly.

"Maybe you'd do better at this." He pulled a pack of cards out of his saddlebag. He fanned the cards and told me to choose one. I did. It was the jack of clubs.

"Now put it back," he said.

I slipped it back into the deck and watched him shuffle the cards. He turned over the top one. The jack of clubs seemed to grin up at me like the stranger. I gasped.

Pa's head whipped up, and he stared at us. "What you doing?" he demanded.

"Pa," I said, still amazed. "Come see this card trick."

Pa scowled. "No time for games," he said shortly. "We got us more important things to do. Go saddle up the horses."

I looked at the stranger and shrugged. He winked at me, and I felt like the sun was rising inside of me with no clouds in sight.

I rolled up my blanket and tied it to the back of my saddle. Then I tossed it onto Blue's back and cinched the girth under her belly. Blue tried to puff out her belly so I wouldn't pull the strap so tight. "Won't work," I told her, laughing and swatting her lightly until she breathed out and I could tighten the girth.

Uncle Leroy wouldn't let no one touch his horse, so I saddled up Pa's horse next, and by the time I was done, the stranger had already saddled his.

Pa gave everyone a cup of coffee he'd boiled over the flames, then he stomped out the fire and we were on our way.

I breathed deep, smelling the coffee, the earth wet with morning dew, and the warmth of the horses. Ma told me that big cities didn't smell like that. She said they smelled like baking bread and gasoline. I scrunched up my nose just thinking of such a combination.

Uncle Leroy led the way. Pa seemed edgy. He kept looking around, twisting in his saddle to look back at me. Then he'd look at the stranger.

As we rode, I caught Pa's eye a time or two, but he didn't smile or wink like the stranger did. He just frowned, his back stiffened, and his knees came in tighter so that Thunder pranced ahead a bit. Then he reined her up and looked at the coming mountains as if he was seeing them for the first time when really I knew he was just waiting for me and the stranger to catch up. Was Pa wondering the same thing as me? Was he comparing me to the stranger? Anyway, him staying so close kept me from asking the stranger any questions, so I bit my tongue and waited.

Uncle Leroy didn't bite his tongue, though. "Were you born here in Oregon? Or somewhere east?"

"Don't remember that far back," the stranger said.

Uncle Leroy ground his teeth like a horse. "And your pa? He still alive?" I saw the frustration in Uncle Leroy's squinty eyes and in the way he lifted his left shoulder up higher than the other.

The stranger looked at him from under the black brim of his hat. "Nobody ever asked after my pa," he said stiffly. "Don't reckon there's any need to."

Uncle Leroy's shoulder hitched up a bit more. "Then what about your ma?"

And the questions went on and on as we rode. The stranger answered every one of them without saying nothing important. I didn't know one dusty inch more about him after the questioning than I did before.

As the sun rose higher and hotter, I pulled off my sweater, careful to keep Ma's locket hidden under my shirt. I didn't know what Pa would do if he saw it, but I didn't reckon it would be good.

I remembered one time Nellie was playing with a piece of red, satin ribbon that had come off one of Ma's city dresses. Pa had snatched it away, and Nellie had bawled her eyes out. He tried to tear the ribbon in two, wrapping it around his hands till it looked like stripes of blood cutting through his fingers, but the ribbon wouldn't tear. Finally he rolled it into a little ball, and with it clenched in his fist he tore out of the house and didn't come back till the next day, smelling like the inside of a bottle. After he'd cleaned himself up, he took Nellie in his arms and told her sorry, even though she had forgotten all about it. He didn't say nothing to me, even though he looked like he wanted to say something. In the end he just walked away.

The heat was so strong that I felt like tucking my hair up under my hat, but I was afraid the silver chain would show. So I had no choice but to let the sun bake my hair. I sipped from my canteen, running the warm, metal-tasting water through my teeth before swallowing. I let a few drops dribble down my chin to wet my shirt, but the water dried faster than it could cool me off.

Uncle Leroy's questions had finally stopped. No use asking questions with no answers. I still had questions for the stranger, but I'd wait till we were alone to ask them.

Around noon we came to a few scrubby trees and stopped for a rest. No one talked. It was too hot. Too hot to eat, even. Pa and Uncle Leroy closed their eyes, tipping their hats over their faces, crossed legs stretched out in front of them. The stranger carefully rolled a cigarette, then he lit it and let the smoke ease between his lips with each breath.

I was too hot to sleep and too young to smoke, and I didn't have enough in my mouth to spit. So I just sat there, squinting out toward the mountains. At first I thought it was only part of the heat waves, tricking my eyes, making me see things that weren't there. I sat forward and looked harder. In the hazy distance the ghost stallion reared up on his hind legs, his head lifted to the sky, his front hooves pawing the air like he was battling a fierce dragon.

I tried not to breathe, afraid I'd alert the others. I wanted to wave my hat to warn the stallion. *Fly away*, I silently screamed. *Go, be free!*

He reared back again, tossing his head, his mane snapping like a flag. Then as suddenly as he was there, he was gone.

I started to breathe again. Sweat cooled my brow and the ridge of my nose. My heart pounded, and I sat back, trying to see the ghost stallion in my mind.

The stranger shifted onto his side. He took a puff of his cigarette, the red glow nearing his fingers. He didn't say nothing. Had he seen the ghost stallion?

My heart filled with hope. Maybe he didn't want to kill the wild horse. Maybe it was just Pa and Uncle Leroy and Mr. Semple who wanted him dead. Me and the stranger could save him.

I wanted to ask him if I was right, but if I said anything, Pa would wake up and demand to know what we were talking about. So I could only ask with my eyes. But I couldn't read his answer.

chapter

We rode on for the rest of the day, the mountains blue in the distance turning gold and green and then violet as the sun sank like the earth was swallowing it whole.

While I tended the horses, Uncle Leroy snared us a rabbit and Pa skinned, spitted, and roasted it over the fire. I couldn't watch. But when the fat started to sputter in the flames, my mouth watered same as the others'. And it sure tasted good even if it was a bit stringy.

After I'd licked all the grease off my fingers, I leaned back against my saddle and cradled a cup of hot coffee in my hands. The night's cool air brushed my face, but the rest of me was warm under my sweater and blanket.

Uncle Leroy kept eyeing the stranger like he was the devil or something. I was ashamed of all the questions Uncle Leroy had been spitting off. Sure, I wanted to know the answers, too, but I knew it wasn't polite to ask outright like that. Ma had taught me better. Seems Pa had learned the same lesson 'cause he barely said a word all day. He just listened, and rode, and kept an eye on me.

I had almost fallen asleep when I heard a wailing sound. I knew it had to be the stranger playing the harmonica since Pa and Uncle Leroy never done nothing more musical than burp in unison.

I peeped around. Even Pa and Uncle Leroy were quiet, their faces drawn out in the flickering firelight. The stranger's hat kept his face in shadow, but his flashing hands, hovering over the spark of silver from the harmonica, looked like moths drawn to a flame.

The stranger played one tune after another, all fitting together like pieces of a large, complicated puzzle. The kind Ma used to fuss over and never finish. Sometimes she'd just sit there and stare at the pieces all afternoon, moving a single piece around the whole table, always looking for a mate.

Finally the last notes faded as the fire burned down to glowing embers. The stranger tucked his harmonica into a hidden pocket, then he leaned back with his head on his saddle, his black eyes staring up at the heavens.

"My ma says you can't see the stars in a big city," I said softly.

He didn't say nothing.

"That's where she come from," I added as if he needed to know. "Said she hated it, though. All the noise and commotion. And she couldn't see the stars none—that's why she came out here. She used to stay out all night sometimes, watching the sky and feeling the earth go round." I sighed.

"So, how'd your ma die?" he asked, his voice quiet and low like he was talking to himself instead of me.

I swallowed hard. "She ain't really dead," I finally said.

He jerked his head around to look at me. He didn't say nothing for a moment, then he asked, "What do you mean?"

I hesitated and squinted over to Pa's side of the fire. His chin was down and his mouth open, so I figured he was asleep.

"She's just gone," I whispered. Seemed awfully strange saying those words out loud for the first time in nine months. "We just say she's dead so Nellie don't go looking for her. And Pa—well, I think he likes to think she's dead rather than just run off. Eases the hurt."

"Who'd she run off with?" he asked.

"What?" Then I lowered my voice, eyeing him sideways. "She didn't go with someone. She was a lady," I said, as if that said it all.

"Where'd she go?"

"I told you she run off. She didn't leave no note or nothing." I had trouble getting the words around the choking lump in my throat. It was just waiting for some salty tears to puff it up big and solid.

I coughed, trying to clear my throat. The stranger just watched me, but Pa jumped to his feet.

"What's the matter?" he demanded, looking over the fire, and I wondered if he'd been asleep at all.

"Nothing," I said, my voice tight and squeaky.

Couldn't see Pa's eyes real good in the dark, but he stood stiff, like a wild animal sniffing the air for his enemy. Didn't know what he'd do next, but finally his shoulders relaxed some and he sat down again, leaning back against his saddle.

The stranger looked at me and winked, then he tipped down his hat and crossed his arms over his chest, and I knew the time for asking and answering questions was over.

I looked up at the stars swirling above my head, knowing I couldn't fall asleep. I wondered if Ma was looking up at the same sky. Did she ever think about me and Nellie and Pa?

Off in the distance I heard a coyote howling, and I felt like howling, too. I felt like lifting my voice to the moon and stars and begging for answers to questions I was too afraid to ask.

The next thing I knew, it was morning and Uncle Leroy was shouting. He kicked up a fuss with his angry words, and clods of dirt with his pointy-toed boots. "You done this to me," he shouted at the stranger.

The stranger hunkered down by the fire, pouring himself a cup of coffee. "I wouldn't give no harm to a horse," he said without even looking up. "To a crazy man, on the other hand . . . " His voice trailed off with meaning.

My uncle raged, his fists clenched, swinging this way and that, hitting nothing but air. He needed Auntie's soothing voice and hands. Meanwhile Jacko's eyes were wide and his nostrils flared open. He kept jerking his head up and laying his ears flat against his head. Pa held his halter lead with both hands, trying to calm him, crooning soft words like a lullaby.

Then I noticed the gash on Jacko's chest and the blood dripping from it.

I jumped to my feet, my blanket falling from my back. "Ho, now, Jacko boy," I said tenderly as I reached out my hand. Jacko tried to rear up, but Pa held him steady.

"Got kicked," Pa said, grunting with the effort of holding the horse still. He nodded toward the stranger. "His horse is shod. Looks bad."

I moved forward smooth and easy, both hands out, reaching for his muzzle. "Hey, boy," I said soft, like it was just me and him in the whole world. He stiffened. I ran my hands gently back and forth over his muzzle and up his jaw to behind his ears.

He snorted, then bobbed his head.

"Come on, boy," I said, "it's okay. You got to let me look at that cut of yours." Real careful, I ran my hands down his neck to his chest. I touched the gash. Jacko shuddered, but he didn't pull away.

My fingers turned slippery with blood as I felt inside the wound to find out how deep the cut ran.

Suddenly the stranger was beside me with a silver flask. He poured some whiskey over the wound to clean it. Jacko whinnied and jerked his head, quivering and huffing with pain and fear.

I took the lead from Pa and reached up to scratch under his forelock. "It's okay, boy, we'll get you fixed up." I wiped the blood with a cloth Pa handed me and pressed it tight to the wound.

"You've got a good hand with horses," the stranger said.

I could feel my face turning pinker than a sunset. "I got it from my pa," I said. "I mean—well, Pa's good with horses, too."

The stranger nodded. "So I saw," he said.

"And—and so are you," I said, stumbling over my words.

For a long moment he just stared at me, and I wished I could know what he was thinking. It seemed as if he was about to say something important, but Pa whirled on us.

"Leroy's taking Jacko back. The horse needs stitches," Pa said brusquely. "Us three'll go on to git the devil horse."

All at once I remembered what we were doing out here and my heart sank into my belly. I imagined the stranger saying, "No, we're going to let that wild horse be, and me and the girl are leaving, going to ride free like the ghost stallion." But the words were only in my head. What the stranger said out loud was, "Then let's go."

c h a p t e r

We left Uncle Leroy behind, cussing under his breath. He couldn't blame the stranger for the kick, which sometimes happened when horses got too close, but he sure tried. In a huff, he said he'd walk toward Mr. Semple's spread, and one of Mr. Semple's hands was sure to see him and get some help.

As we rode off, clouds gathered up ahead. At first they were just wisps of cotton, but then they puffed up like mushrooms, blocking out the sun.

Lightning forked the sky up over the mountains, and the smell of rain swept down over us. Blue side-stepped at the boom of thunder, so I leaned forward and rubbed her ears, murmuring soft till she calmed down.

"We should find some shelter," the stranger said. "Storm's going to be on us soon."

Pa tipped back his head, holding on to his hat so it didn't blow off. "We've got time," he said. "Besides, the storm's going north. It'll miss us."

The stranger shook his head. "Ain't so," he said. "Coming straight here. Need to find us some low ground out of the weather."

"We'll lose the trail," Pa argued. "I got to get me that horse before he ruins me." He kicked his horse into a canter.

I knew if I didn't get to the ghost stallion first, Pa would surely kill him. I charged ahead into the wind, into the storm, galloping past the stranger and Pa.

I heard shouting behind me, but I didn't slow. Then someone was riding alongside me. It was Pa. He reached out a hand and grabbed the bridle on my horse, pulling us to a jerky stop.

"Are you crazy, girl?" he demanded. "You can't charge off like the devil's chasing you. You could get killed."

I was breathing heavy, like I was the one who was running.

"You could lame your horse. Don't you ever think?" His face blazed red with fury.

"That's all you care about," I screamed back. "Your damn horses!"

"That ain't true."

"Is too," I cried, "and you know it."

"Don't you talk to me like that." He wrenched the bridle, pulling me closer so our knees rubbed together. "I'm your pa whether you like it or not, and you'll do as I say."

It was in me to yell back at him, to scream and shriek and defy him like a storm all my own. I wasn't his daughter, and he knew it. I knew it. Anybody who looked at us with one eye knew it. But when I opened my mouth to tell him so, the wind snatched the words right out of me, leaving me empty.

The stranger joined us, his hat held around his neck with a leather thong. His black hair with the curling ends whipped about his face.

Pa stared at the both of us like he was just noticing our hair and how our noses slanted the same way. I tugged at the silver chain wrapped around my neck, pulling the heart locket free from my hair and sweater.

Pa stiffened to see it. He held rigid like he was face-to-face with a rattler, daring it to strike, praying it wouldn't.

"Where'd you get that?" he choked out. "Tell me right now," he shouted when I didn't say anything right off.

"Ma gave it to me," I lied. "Said it was special."

"Give it here."

I shook my head. "It's mine."

He reached for it.

At that moment the stranger pointed. "There he is," he said.

We all looked. The ghost stallion tossed his head at us and screamed a warning. The sound sank right into my bones.

"Let's go!" Pa shouted, forgetting about me and the locket. He rode off, pulling his rifle free of its sheath.

The stranger squeezed his knees and his horse bolted, too, leaving me in their wake. I watched the ghost stallion gallop off after his mares, his tail flagging proudly.

Pa got off a wild shot. Digging my heels into Blue's sides, I leaned low over her neck as we charged forward, the wind pushing against us.

We were on three strong horses and moving fast. The ghost stallion had to watch over his brood, some of them swollen with foals on the way and others looking out for their yearlings. We got closer and closer.

Ahead I saw the stallion stop, and I knew he had reached the river, wide and deep. He could turn north or south and keep running, but we'd catch him eventually, what with his mares and yearlings slowing him down.

Or he could try to cross the raging river. If he made it, he'd be free. With one last toss of his head, he plunged into the water and his band followed.

We reached the muddy bank just as the last of the mares were struggling up the other side. Two mares and a yearling didn't make it. I could still see their heads, like small logs, bobbing down the river until they were swept under.

Pa shook his gun at the outlaw horse. "I'll git you," he screamed, fighting with the wind to be heard.

The ghost stallion faced us and reared in defiance. Pa brought the gun up, sighting down the barrel. The stallion was too close. The river was wide, but not wide enough.

"No!" I shouted. I kicked my horse forward, ramming into Pa and upsetting his mount. Startled, Pa jerked in the saddle, trying to regain his balance, his rifle whipping every which way. Suddenly it went off and I heard the bullet shriek by my ear. I screamed.

Pa's face went dead white. He dropped his gun and reached for me. I pulled back on the reins and felt Blue slide in the mud. Someone grabbed me, clutching my sweater and nearly strangling me. Blue struggled to get her footing, but it was no good. She kicked once, the hands trying to hold me slid away, and Blue and I plunged into the icy cold river.

c h a p t e r 8

The cold water squeezed the breath right out of me. I gasped for air but only got a mouthful of water. Coughing and choking, I kicked my legs free of the stirrups, barely able to keep my head above water. I splashed and slapped the surface, trying to remember how to swim. Drowning seemed so easy.

I saw Blue in the distance. With her neck stretched out she made for the left bank. She finally pulled herself free of the river, clambering up the steep, muddy side. Then the river pulled and twirled me in another direction till I thought I'd rip apart at the joints. Sometimes it sucked me under to where it was quiet and calmer. But then along came a rock, ramming into me, throwing me back up to the air, back into the living.

I kicked off my boots and tried to drag my sweater over my head, but it clung to me tight. Swirling in the currents, images flashed through my head. Ma dancing around the room with me in her arms. Nellie jumping into Pa's wide-open arms. Pa raging and snorting and spitting the day Ma left. The river tossed me along, knocking memories around like they didn't have no meaning.

After a while the river finally calmed. It still ran fast, but the water looked smooth, and no boulders broke its surface. I felt heavy as a dead cow, and I was just barely able to keep my eyes and nose above water, gasping for air when I could. Now Smoky's Canyon rose up on either side of me as the river pulled me along. Pa and the stranger were well out of sight.

My legs cramped from the cold, and every time I tried to breathe, I took in more water than air. It felt like I had rocks tied to my ankles, trying to pull me down for good.

Then I remembered the ghost stallion, and I prayed he got away. Would Pa go after the devil horse or me? I let my head dip under the water so's I didn't have to think on the answer. I held my breath as long as I could, waiting for my lungs to burst and fill with water. But something inside me raised my head at the last moment, and I got a gulp of air instead of the Smoky River. I figured I would have to try to make it to shore because my body wasn't ready to give up yet.

Slowly I aimed myself across the current, but I couldn't feel my feet, and my hands were frozen into claws.

I should've remembered where the river twisted and turned and dropped, but all I could think about was taking one more kick, one more stroke. So when the distant sound of falling water reached me, I thought it was just blood rushing through my ears.

Then I remembered.

I looked up at the canyon walls and spotted the Old Man's Nose. I knew if I was on that cliff and looked south, I'd be able to see the Smoky Falls not too far off. From down here, I couldn't see nothing, but I could hear the falls getting louder, and my heart pumping harder, and my teeth chattering with cold.

They were always finding dead things in the pool at the bottom of the falls. Nothing survived the brutal Smoky Falls.

Ahead I saw the beginning of rapids. I stroked harder, kicking my numb legs to reach the side of the river. My frozen hands were barely any use.

The canyon walls narrowed, forcing the river faster and faster. Then I saw it. Just before the rapids, water and time had worn away a cove in the solid rock wall. It was my last chance to save myself.

I forced my hands to paddle like a dog's. Suddenly there was no push or pull trying to rip my body from its course, just a gentle lapping. I couldn't feel the pebbles and rocks beneath my numb feet, but I knew they were there because when I stopped kicking, I didn't sink. My tired legs pushed me forward until I could crawl on my hands and knees and keep my head above water at the same time.

Slowly I pulled myself out of the freezing water. Then I collapsed, aching in every part of my body. I was too exhausted to check for blood or broken bones. I could barely move. It was hard enough just to breathe.

———

I curled up tight on my side. The air was warmer than the ice-melted Smoky, and my hands started to tingle painfully.

I don't know how long I lay there, but when I awoke, I thought I was drowning, only it was the storm drowning me in rain, not the river.

I pulled myself farther into the cove, where tall grass and small trees had taken hold on the rocky land. Hardly any wind made it into this sheltered place, so the rain drove straight down, like it was digging for the far side of the earth. All I could hear was the hammering rain and the constant roar of the falls in the background.

I checked both arms and legs for bloody gashes. I had one on my right elbow, but the blood was slow and it was more a scrape since the rock had to cut through a sweater and flannel shirt first. There was a welt on my thigh I could feel under my jeans. It was sore to the touch, so I left it alone. I was sure it would be a big, purple flower when I got around to looking at it.

I didn't know I wasn't alone until I heard a loud snuffling sound right behind me. I jerked around, my heart catching.

The ghost stallion stared back at me.

Just barely through the rain, I could see his mares clustered behind him, heads low. The stallion scratched the ground and tossed his head. Slowly I stood up and reached a hand forward, forgetting my bruises and pains. Closer and closer. His muzzle quivered. Then with a flick of his tail, he turned and pranced away before I could even graze a finger over his whiskers.

I laughed, part in fear, part in joy. Wild horses could trample someone to death if they had a mind to, and this horse was an outlaw. I couldn't be safe so close to him, yet I didn't want to be anywhere else.

I sat down again and watched the ghost stallion. He huddled his mares tighter, and then stood apart from them, alone. But he was free. No brand marked his flank. No halter had worn patches of hair off his face. No saddle had left sores and bumps. Instead, scars crisscrossed his chest and legs, maybe from barbed wire fences. And one long gash was just healing on his right shoulder. Freedom scars.

I reached up to clutch the locket strung around my neck, but all I got was a handful of soggy sweater. I looked down, feeling through my clothes, reaching under my shirt, combing fingers through the knots of my hair. But it was gone. My mother's silver heart . . . my father's lock of hair.

Pressing my hands to my chest, I felt the heavy beat of my own heart. Without the locket I had no proof of who I was. I had no me.

chapter  9

I settled under a tree, trying to keep out of the rain, hoping the lightning would stay up in the mountains and not find my little cove. The stallion watched me the whole time, but he didn't flinch.

The rest of the day passed dark because of the storm and the high walls of the canyon around us. I huddled up against the trunk of the tree and wondered how the outlaw and his mares had gotten down here, but I couldn't see well enough to find a path in the steep walls. My leaving would have to wait till the storm blew over.

With my knees pulled up, I watched the ghost stallion, hardly believing I was seeing him so close. He stood proud, even in the drenching rain. While all his mares hung their heads, he kept his high. It was easy to tell he'd never been broken.

I remembered the silver heart I lost in the river. Gone forever. Soon as I could leave, I'd go find the stranger. I'd just come right out and ask who he was and what he was doing here. I'd ask my questions straight and not give up till I got answers true.

But for now it was just me and the stallion, him looking ghostly in the rain and fog that separated us. I wanted to stare at him forever, but pretty soon it was too dark to see anything. I should have been afraid out there all alone at night, but knowing the stallion was close by made me feel safe for some reason.

My forehead dipped to my knees when I couldn't keep my eyes open anymore. The rain was now just mist. I shivered and coughed. At least the air wasn't cold like I expected, so I wasn't too miserable, sleeping on the hard earth with stones and sticks for my bed.

I woke up only once in the middle of the night. I couldn't see nothing because clouds still hung heavy in the sky and covered the moon, but I felt the ghost stallion standing over me like I was one of his foals.

In the morning the sky still looked angry, but the rain had stopped. The mares were ready to go, pawing the ground and shifting restlessly. I recognized seven of Pa's horses. Bessy, one that just got taken the other night, nickered to me when I said her name.

I stood up stiffly, feeling all the bumps and bruises I couldn't see. A coughing fit grabbed my chest and wouldn't let go. I bent double, trying to breathe without hacking. The stallion backed off a couple of steps, watching me and sniffing the air. When I finally stopped coughing, I held out my hand to Bessy, who eased forward and blew into my palm, rubbing her nose against my skin like she was looking for a treat.

"Hey, girl," I said softly. A plan formed as I moved my hand to her ears, touching easy until she pressed against my hand for some more scratching. I laughed, but not too hard. I didn't want to start coughing again.

Still scratching her, I ran my hand up and down her neck, tugging on her mane. She didn't sidestep.

Taking a breath, I firmly grabbed two hands of mane and pulled myself onto her back. She shifted slightly at the added weight, but that's all she protested.

"Good girl," I murmured as I glanced at the stallion. He didn't look like he was about to charge me and knock me off his new mare—he just snorted and turned away. His snort reminded me of Pa, and I wondered what Pa was doing. Was he out looking for me? Had he raced home to set up a search party, thinking I drowned in the river? Or was he still tracking the outlaw?

The stallion led the way to the rear of the cove and behind a big boulder that must have slid from the cliff during a long-ago storm. His mares followed one by one. That's when I saw the path. It was well worn and very steep. I was happy to be going up it instead of down.

Bessy's muscles bunched and stretched on the climb. Only once did her foot slip, and for a second my stomach lurched as I waited for the fall. But Bessy recovered her footing on the narrow trail, and before long we made it to the top.

As soon as we passed over the edge, Bessy broke into a canter to catch up with the others. I thought my bones would break apart after my wild ride down the Smoky River, but I just clenched my teeth and hung on.

The ghost stallion led the way along the ridge that would lead down from Smoky's Canyon, away from the mountains, over the plains. Almost like he was taking me home.

I leaned low over Bessy's neck, hanging on tight with my thighs and my hands on her mane. She was pure stock and a strong runner. We moved into a gallop as we eased down the ridge onto the meadows. She pressed on, passing the others until she was catching up to the ghost stallion himself. He could have pressed on faster and left us far behind, but he let us catch up till we were straining neck and neck.

I couldn't help the pounding of my heart or the smile that bared my teeth to the wind. I never felt so free, racing with the ghost stallion at my side. This is how I wanted my life to be. Free to go anywhere with nothing holding me back.

We raced on. The land swayed and dipped with shallow valleys and gentle swells. We crested one hill, then plummeted down the other side only to face the next easy rise, me leaving a blazing trail of laughter behind us.

On and on we galloped, sweat darkening Bessy's hide, while the ghost stallion looked like he could run for days and never slow down. We were just nearing the top of a hill when the world turned upside down.

Pa and the stranger charged at us. They must have been hidden by the hill, and now they were practically alongside us. For one second I smiled, proud to be seen with the ghost stallion, riding free like the wind, but the next second my heart tumbled deep into the earth.

Pa shouted, "Yeeha!" to his horse and whirled a lasso above his head. We had raced right into a trap. Pa had seen us coming, but we hadn't seen him.

Pa threw his lasso, catching the stallion clean and tight, the other end wrapped around his saddle horn. The outlaw reared and screamed with anger, trying to fight off his attackers with striking hooves.

Tugging back on Bessy's mane, I yelled, "Ho, girl!" She jerked to a sudden stop. I flew through the air, landing hard on my backside, pain shooting up my spine, the breath knocked out of me. Hooves pounded the ground. By now the other mares had caught up, wanting to stay with their stallion but confused and frightened.

The stallion still screamed, pulling on the rope, fighting to get free, but Pa held on dear like he wasn't going to lose this battle nohow.

The stallion sighted me on the ground, helpless. His eyes flamed red, and he charged right for me. I couldn't move. I knew it was all my fault he was caught. I had run him into the trap. I deserved his hatred even though it broke my heart to see it.

I heard shouting, but I couldn't make out the words. Pa jerked on the lasso to stop him, but the wild stallion just pulled forward, heading right for me.

Then a strong arm reached down and scooped me up. Before I knew it, the stranger held me close in his arms in front of his saddle and we were out of the stallion's way. Pa heaved on the rope, pulling the wild horse around.

The stranger didn't say nothing. Didn't need to. He had saved my life. And Pa finally had what he wanted.

chapter 10

Over my head the stranger threw his lasso. Now both he and Pa had ahold of the ghost stallion. The wild horse didn't have a chance.

Pa had the stallion tight on the end of his rope, jerking and tugging on it, yanking when the stallion stiffened his legs and wouldn't move 'cept to be dragged. And that's what Pa and the stranger did. They pulled and fought the ghost stallion all the rest of the day. I couldn't watch. It was bad enough listening to the anger and terror coming from the horse, his snorts and shrieks, and curses coming from Pa. The stranger did his battling in silence.

By nightfall the ghost stallion knew he had lost the fight. My heart ached, but there was nothing I could do for him. Not yet.

We rode through the night, me nodding off between my fits of coughing, only to awaken to find the stranger's arms holding me safe and warm.

By dawn we were close to home. Uncle Leroy came out to meet us soon as we could see the rails of the outer pastures. He rode up, telling us that Jacko was stitched up in the stable and no fever or infection had set in and that old Blue had galloped in just a couple hours ago. Then he looked at me.

"What happened to you? You look like a drowned rat."

I was too tired and discouraged to bite back. Anyway, Pa gave him a look and Uncle Leroy shut up. I noticed his shoulders were even. Auntie had soothed him down like I knew she would, only it didn't take much to rile him up again.

"When are you going to deliver the tail?" the stranger asked Pa.

I shuddered, feeling stupid for thinking that maybe the stranger was going to help save the stallion in the end, like one of the heroes from the Western novels Ma used to read to me.

"Wait till it's dark," Pa said.

I knew why. Pa knew what he was doing was wrong, and he didn't want no one to see him do it. Things done in the dark seem like maybe they're not real. At least that's how I figured Pa was seeing it.

When we got home, the stranger let me down and then helped Pa and Uncle Leroy pen the wild horse in our sturdiest corral. Even still, the stallion bucked and reared, trying to pull the cross-bars apart.

The rope Pa had used to bring in the outlaw hung over the rail. Blood streaked one end, and I looked at the horse for red around his neck till I realized the blood was on Pa's end. Must have rubbed his hands raw bringing in his prize. I was glad of his pain, for the stinging and burning in his palms. He deserved it for what he'd done. For what he was going to do when the sun went down.

Nellie, wearing a dress the color of a yellow butterfly, ran out soon as she heard us. "Oh, Pa," she cried, clapping, "you brung in the devil horse."

Pa swung her up in his arms. "We got us the devil horse and our mares back, and a nice reward from Bones."

Nellie squealed with delight as he rubbed his whiskered face into her soft neck. He laughed and twirled her round once before putting her down.

The stallion's mares had followed him here, and now Pa and Leroy herded them into a pasture so's they could separate Pa's from Mr. Semple's.

Nellie danced in circles, chanting, "The devil horse, the devil horse, we got ourselves the devil horse." She grabbed my hand and tried to pull me into one of our dances, but I jerked away.

I glared at her. "He's not a devil, so you just shut your mouth." I pretended I didn't care that her lower lip trembled and her eyes filled with tears at my harsh words. Half of me wanted to hug her up tight and say I was sorry, but the meaner half made my heart clench just as tight as my jaw.

She turned to the stranger, who stood near us, one black boot resting on the lowest rail, his hat pulled over his forehead.

"He is the devil, ain't he mister?" She tugged on his shirt when he didn't answer right off.

I wanted him to say he weren't a devil but just a free spirit who needed and deserved to be wild and running loose with the wind. But he just said, "I don't reckon it matters much anymore." Then he started to pull a pink scarf out of Nellie's boot. "Well, looky here," he said. "What's this?"

Nellie stared in amazement as the stranger pulled out more and more of the long scarf. Finally the end came free, and he tied it around her neck like she was some kind of present. She smiled at him so big, but I reckoned he was used to that. With all his magic, he probably got whatever he wanted.

I glanced at the ghost stallion. The horse turned to me and I saw the look in his eyes, fierce and crazed. His nostrils blew in and out with each heavy breath. His stare was mean, like he wanted to kill.

"I'm sorry," I said, my voice cracked from all the coughing and raspy from the heat that started to pound in my head.

"What you sorry for?" Nellie asked, draping herself over the lower rails so she could look into the small corral.

"I'm sorry for everything."

"Are you talking to the horse?"

I wondered about that. Who was I talking to? I

glanced over Nellie's head to the stranger. His head was turned my way, but I couldn't tell if he was looking at me or Nellie or the mountains in the distance.

Nellie scrambled to the top rail. The ghost stallion pawed the dirt from the other side of the corral. "Look," she said, "he likes me." She reached forward. "Come here, devil horse, come here," she called.

"Leave him alone," I warned. But too late.

The stallion reared. Nellie screamed, lost her balance, and fell forward. She caught herself on one of the lower rails and broke her fall before landing on her side.

The ghost stallion charged at her.

My heart near exploded. Next thing I knew, I was inside the corral, crouching by Nellie. I held up my arms, waving them back and forth. "Ho," I cried, but he didn't even hesitate, just kept coming, only now he was heading straight for me.

"Get out," I shouted, hoping Nellie knew I was talking to her. I couldn't turn my head to see.

I waited for the stallion's crushing force to land on my head and shoulders. Suddenly a whip flicked out and stung the wild horse on the neck, and he whirled to see where the attack had come from. An arm grabbed me around the middle and flung me over the rail. I crashed on the other side, falling more on my shoulder than anywhere else. Pain shot across my back and up my neck.

"What the hell were you doing, girl?" Pa demanded, jumping down off the rail next to me. "Did you think you'd break him?" He gripped my arm and yanked me to my feet. "That horse would sooner kill you than look at you! I didn't hunt for you all night only to bring you back here to be trampled to death."

He took a big breath like he wanted to say more, then he just shook me hard and let go. He spun around to see Nellie in tears in the stranger's arms. Throwing the whip to the ground, Pa rushed forward and grabbed Nellie into his own arms. "You leave her be," he shouted to the stranger. "This here's my daughter! Keep yer hands off, y'hear?" Holding Nellie tight, Pa swept back to the house.

It was like all the air had been sucked out of us. Uncle Leroy, who had watched the whole thing with a shaking head, disappeared into the barn. Just me and the stranger was left. Me staring at him; him staring at the ghost stallion.

"You should have told him what happened," he said. "That you were trying to save your sister."

"He wouldn't have listened," I muttered.

The stranger led his horse over to the trough to feed and water it. I followed him and looked around. We were alone. This was what I'd been waiting for.

I took a deep breath. "Who are you?"

He didn't even look up.

I tried again. "Why'd you come here?"

Still he said nothing.

"At least can I come with you when you go?" I asked.

"And leave Nellie and the horses?" he said as if I never asked those other questions.

"I can find horses somewhere else. And Nellie . . ." My voice trailed off. "I'd come back and visit her."

The stranger bent down to pick his horse's hooves. "And what would you do if you didn't eat here, sleep here?"

"I'd be free."

The stranger laughed shortly. "Free to do what?"

"Free like you," I said, leaning forward. "Free to go wherever I want, do whatever I want."

For a long moment he said nothing, just dug dirt and rocks out of the hoof between his knees. Finally he wiped a trickle of sweat off his cheek and said, "I don't think your pa would like that much."

"He ain't my pa."

There. I'd said it. Only I didn't feel no freer. I didn't feel like my soul was lifted to the sky for finally saying the truth out loud.

"Git inside, girl," Pa called from the porch. His voice made me jump.

I didn't understand my heart at that moment. I told myself I didn't care if Pa had overheard me. But something hurt inside me more than I ever felt before.

I looked one more time at the stranger, but it was like he had never heard me. Slowly I walked to the house. I noticed Mr. Semple's red truck driving off. He must have come and settled with Pa, knowing he'd get the stallion's tail soon enough.

Inside, Auntie was bustling around the kitchen. She sure could move quick for a large woman.

She turned to me and threw up her hands. "You look terrible!"

Her loud voice rang in my ears and made me wince. My whole body ached, inside and out, and I suddenly felt too weak to even cough. I just stood there. Must have looked like one of my old rag dolls with the stuffing coming out, 'cause Auntie pulled me close into her arms and near suffocated me with her hug.

"You poor dear," she murmured. Then she helped me up to my room, stripped off my damp clothes, and tucked me into bed.

With a promise of some hot soup, she waddled out and clomped down to the kitchen. I just stared up at the ceiling, too tired to move, too tired to think.

Later, when I heard the click of heels on the floor outside my room, I thought it was Auntie come with my soup. Only it wasn't.

Pa stood in my doorway, his head bowed, his hat in his hands. He still had his boots on, which told me he wasn't planning on staying long.

He cleared his throat. "How you feeling?"

"Not too bad," I lied. My voice sounded squeaky.

"You trying to sleep?" he asked.

"Not yet."

He took one step into the room, for the first time that I could remember. "I have something to tell you."

I nodded like I knew what he was talking about.

He cleared his throat again. "It's about your ma."

My heart clenched up at his words.

"Your ma, she made me promise never to tell you. . . ." He took a deep breath. "But I don't reckon it matters now. Or maybe it matters more," he added after a pause.

"What, Pa?"

He pulled up the rickety old chair I kept in the corner and sat on the edge, elbows resting on his knees. Still he kept his head bowed so I only saw the top of his hair, matted down with dried sweat.

"It's an old story," he started, "but it's the truth, and I want you to hear it." He worked the brim of his hat around in his hands as he talked. "I met your ma at a rodeo. I was riding for Mr. Semple, before I started training his horses. Your ma was there in the stands, looking like a rose, so pretty next to all those thorny cowboys."

I nodded, like I heard this story before. But the truth was, Ma never told me how she met Pa.

"After I won, your ma came up to me and started talking. I hardly knew what to say to her. I could tell by her talk that she come from a city. I didn't know what she wanted from me.

"We talked some. She did most of the talking, but she said she liked how I listened. You know I ain't much of a talker."

I did know, and I could hardly believe he was talking so much right now, telling me a story I wasn't sure I even wanted to hear.

"So she talked and I listened, and before I knew it, I asked her to marry me and she said yes."

I must have looked a sight at that moment with my mouth hanging open. "Didn't you court her none? You just went and asked her the minute you met her? And she said yes?" I knew I was just repeating what he already said, but I couldn't help myself.

He nodded. "Then she told me about you."

My breath stopped halfway out.

"But it didn't make no difference to me," he went on quickly. "I said I'd take you as my own. And I tried."

It was like all Pa's words were balloons floating over my head. But I didn't have the energy to reach up and grab them before they floated away.

"Every time I looked at you, though, I couldn't help but think of *him*. Maybe if you had looked more like your ma, I wouldn't have done so much thinking and wishing. . . ." He ran a hand through his stiff hair, standing it up in spikes. "I know she tried to tell him about you. Wrote letters, she told me, but she stopped after we married."

"How come Ma never told me?" I whispered.

Finally he looked at me good, his eyes not flicking away like they usually did. "She was ashamed," he said flatly.

"But all those years," I said, my voice choking with anger, "I wondered about me and my dark hair. Ma used to laugh skittish and say God dipped my head into mud so I wouldn't shine brighter than he did. I always knew, though," I said after a long moment of just breathing. "I always knew."

Pa pulled something out of his pocket and handed it to me.

"I pulled this off your neck when I was trying to keep you from falling into the Smoky. I reckon your ma would have wanted you to have it. And anything else you find in the attic that you want." He stood up abruptly. "It scared me half to death when I almost shot you. What made you do such a crazy fool thing, getting in my way like that?"

"I didn't want you to shoot the ghost stallion," I said, fingering the locket.

Pa snorted and wiped his nose with the back of his hand. "But I could have killed you." He pressed his fingers against his closed eyelids and took a deep breath. When he looked at me again, his eyes were red.

"Please don't kill the ghost stallion," I blurted out. I didn't think it would do no good, but I had to ask.

Pa said nothing for a moment. Then he shook his head. "With him free, my mares ain't safe, and without my mares, I have no work."

I had known he wouldn't change his mind, and I was mad at myself for even hoping.

He moved to the door. "Evelyn said to let you sleep."

"Pa?"

He stopped, but he didn't turn around.

"Why'd you tell me about Ma?"

Still with his back to me, he said, "Time for the truth to come out. Secrets just make a heart heavy, and I reckon our hearts are heavy enough."

With his head bowed, Pa left the room.

I dangled the heart locket in front of my eyes, thinking about everything. The truth, he'd said. But he still hadn't told me the one thing I wanted to hear. I refastened the clasp, hooking it where it wasn't broken, and slipped the chain over my head. I shivered as the cold metal took a moment to warm to my skin.

Outside, I heard the shrill whinny of the ghost stallion. I only had one chance to set him free. Tonight I'd set us both free.

chapter 12

The loud crack of a gun sounded in my dream. I awoke with a start. Maybe I was too late. I tumbled out of bed, wincing at my stiff shoulder, and threw on some clothes.

Outside, clouds scuttled across the moon. The wind picked the hair off my back and cooled my fever sweat. I ran on wobbly legs toward the corral, praying the ghost stallion was still alive.

Hurrying, I nearly bumped into Pa on the rail.

"What are you doing out here?" he asked, his voice harsh.

I flinched, not sure if I dared try to defy him face-to-face. My fever had left me weak and tired, but I stood up straighter, relieved to see the ghost stallion still alive in the corral.

"You should be in bed," Pa argued. "You're still sick."

The sound of a rifle being cocked interrupted us. We both turned and faced the stranger.

"Time to ride on," the stranger said, standing there. "But first I want what's coming to me."

Pa didn't even hesitate. "You can't have her," he said fiercely.

Silence hung in the air like a veil of smoke. My heart thudded at Pa's words.

The stranger chuckled. "You mistook my meaning, mister. I just want my reward."

"No," I cried, brushing by Pa. I grabbed the stranger's arm that held the rifle. "You can't kill him. Set him free. Please," I begged.

The stranger shook my arm loose. When he lifted the rifle again, I lunged for him, trying to knock him off his feet, but he just shrugged me aside and I fell on my sore shoulder.

Pa blew up like I never seen him before. He pushed the stranger and they tumbled to the ground. I was afraid the gun would go off, but Pa wrestled the rifle out of the stranger's hands and flung it wide. They kept fighting till I couldn't tell Pa from the stranger, they were so mixed up, a jumble of curses and blows and grunts of pain.

The ghost stallion reared and whinnied in his corral, snapping his head up and down. I ran to the gate and lifted the crossbars. "Heeya!" I cried, waving my hands. "Go on, get out of here. Go free!"

The horse bolted for freedom, taking the path between the corrals and outer pastures. Now was my chance to race after him and set myself free.

"Hey," the stranger shouted. I whirled around. He jumped up, grabbed his rifle, and lifted it to sight down the barrel, but the stallion was too far away. Pa lay on the ground, curled up tight like a baby.

The stranger mounted his horse and thundered after the ghost stallion, the rifle held high in his right hand.

I crouched beside Pa, who was groaning. "Are you okay?"

He just tensed with pain, then gasped out, "Go get him."

I didn't know what he meant. Go get the stallion so's he could kill him, or go get the stranger for some reason? But I had my own reasons for going.

I ran to the stables and led out Rider, my legs weak and shaky. Grabbing hold of his mane, I tried to pull myself onto his bare back. Took me three tries. My arms were quivering from the effort. Finally I got up, kicking him straight into a gallop. Keeping low over his neck, I gripped his sides with my knees and kept my hands tangled in his mane. In the scattered moon glow I saw the stranger far ahead of me, but no ghost stallion.

The pounding of the hooves below me worked into my chest, throbbing in time to my heartbeat. I knew it was dangerous to ride so wild in the dark. If Rider landed in a hole, he'd snap a leg and have to be put down, and I might break my neck. But I had to catch up—I couldn't stop or even slow down.

Ahead, the stranger wheeled in a circle. He had the ghost stallion on the other end of his lasso. I charged closer, praying he didn't get a chance to shoot the horse before I got there.

The wild horse bucked, twisting and turning like a tornado.

Finally close enough, I slid off Rider and stumbled forward. "Stop it," I shouted. "You have to let him go."

The stranger didn't say anything, just jerked the rope, winding it around his saddle horn so his hands would be free to shoot.

"No!" I screamed. "Let him go!" I ran closer and pounded on his leg.

Still the stranger ignored me. He lifted his rifle and aimed.

A shot rang out cold and hard. Frozen, I waited for the ghost stallion to fall to his knees and crumple, but instead the stranger dropped the nose of his rifle, swinging around to look over my head, and I realized the shot had come from another gun.

Pa's voice came solid and strong. "Let the stallion go." He aimed his rifle at the stranger.

"Pa!" I yelled.

"What the hell are you doing?" the stranger demanded, cutting me off. "I was promised one hundred dollars to kill this horse, and I aim on collecting."

Pa dug into his pocket and held out a wad of paper. "Here's your money. Now let the stallion free like the girl asked."

The stranger hesitated, then shrugged like it didn't matter to him whether the ghost stallion lived or died—he just wanted the money. He loosened the lasso and flicked it over the horse's head. The wild horse charged off, looking more ghostly than ever in the moonlight.

The stranger came forward, his hand held out for the money. Pa grabbed his arm. "Don't never pass through here again, y'hear?"

The stranger yanked the money and his arm out of Pa's grip. He tucked the bills into one of his pockets and pulled the hat back on his head. Then he turned to me. "You still want to come?"

I glanced at Pa. He held stiff in his saddle.

"Where you going?" I asked the stranger.

He waved a hand toward the mountains. "Any-where," he said.

I looked at Pa again. Now he wasn't rigid like a sol-dier, but slumped in his saddle, his head down, not looking at me.

"Pa?" I said.

He slowly lifted his head. "Don't go," were his only words.

All the magic and dreams and wishes in the world

couldn't tempt me no more. I turned to the stranger and shook my head.

He took one hard look at me with his black eyes. "Don't you want to know who I am?"

"Don't matter no more," I said.

The stranger wheeled his horse and rode off, never once looking back.

———

Pa swung down off his horse and took a step toward me. "You sure this is what you want?"

I tried to answer, but a big ball stuck in my throat and a wash of rain fell on my cheeks. Only there was no storm, and I realized it wasn't rain soaking my face, but my own tears. I let them fall, a river of grief and longing washing away at last. Tears I had held fast for so long. Tears that burned my nose and stung my eyes. Real tears.

"Mary Elizabeth," Pa said, his voice scratchy like he hadn't said those words in so long and he didn't know how they'd come out.

I nodded. Not *girl*. *Mary Elizabeth*. My name. Ma's name.

"Think Ma will ever come back?" I asked softly, looking at the silver locket around my neck.

"Might so," he said, then he considered for a long moment. "But I doubt it. She's looking for something she never found."

"I was looking, too," I said.

"All of us are searching for something, I figure," Pa said. "But it's the lucky ones who find it."

"I reckon so," I agreed. I opened the locket. The black hair quivered a moment, then a breeze picked it up and tossed it into the night. Gone, like the ghost stallion. All that was left was a silver heart, waiting to be filled with something else, a new bit of a dream, a different wish, a better hope. I snapped it closed and dropped it under my shirt.

Pa reached forward and pulled me into his arms, and it was like we were working horses together and didn't need no words between us.

DATE DUE